Dora's Easter Basket

adapted by Sarah Willson
from the screenplay by Eric Weiner
Illustrated by Susan Hall

SCHOLASTIC INC.
New York Toronto London Auckland Sydney
Mexico City New Delhi Hong Kong Buenos Aires

Based on the TV series *Dora the Explorer*® as seen on Nick Jr.®

No part of this publication may be reproduced in whole or in part, or stored in a retrieval system, or transmitted in any form or by any means, electronic, mechanical, photocopying, recording, or otherwise, without written permission of the publisher. For information regarding permission, write to Simon Spotlight, Simon & Schuster Children's Publishing Division, 1230 Avenue of the Americas, New York, NY 10020.

ISBN 0-439-46254-1

12 11 10 9 8 7 6 5 4 3   3 4 5 6 7 8/0

Printed in the U.S.A.

First Scholastic printing, March 2003

Say it in Spanish!

Hola: OH-la

Vámonos: VA-mo-nos

Buenos Días: BWEH-nos DEE-ahs

Muy Bien: MWEE Bee-YEN

Uno: OO-no

Dos: DOHs

Tres: TREHs

Cuatro: KWAH-troh

Cinco: SING-koh

Seis: SAYs

Siete: See-EH-tay

Ocho: OH-cho

Nueve: New-EH-vay

Diez: Dee-EHZ

Once: ON-say

Doce: DOH-say

¡Hola! I'm Dora. Boots and I are going on an egg hunt. Mami and Papi hid twelve special eggs for us to find.

Each egg has a prize inside. The big, yellow egg has the largest prize of all. Will you help us find all twelve eggs?

Where should we look for the eggs? Let's ask the Map! Say, "Map!"
The Map says we should look for eggs by the Duck Pond and at the Farm. Then we should search for the big, yellow egg at Grandma's House. Come on! ¡Vámonos!

Do you see any eggs? Where?

How many eggs do we have?

We have to watch out for Swiper the fox. He'll try to swipe our eggs. If you see him, say, "Swiper, no swiping!"

We stopped Swiper! Thanks for helping. Let's see what prizes are inside our eggs.

Can you tell which prizes came from which eggs?
Map told us to look near the Duck Pond. Do you see the pond?

We made it to the Duck Pond. Look! There's a *Mami* duck and her ducklings. How many eggs do you see?

Uh-oh. How are we going to get the eggs off those lily pads?

Let's check Backpack. Backpack always has everything we need.

Can you find something in Backpack that will help us scoop up those eggs?

The net worked! Good job! Wow, look at the prizes that were inside the eggs. Can you tell which prize came from which egg?

Do you see another egg? Oh, it's on the sleepy sloth's tummy! We have to wake her up and ask for the egg. Can you help us? We need to use Spanish to wake her up. Can you say, "*Buenos días*"?

You did it! She gave us the egg. See the prize that was inside? You wind it up to make it go. Uh-oh, it's rolling away. Follow that car!

Can you find the path
that leads to the Farm?

Here's our friend Tico the squirrel. ¡Hola, Tico! Tico says we'll find one egg next to an animal that says, "oink," and one egg next to an animal that says, "moo."

Great job! Tico says there is one more egg to find at the Farm. Do you see it? Show Tico the way to the egg.

He got there! Great! ¡Muy bien!

Let's see the prizes inside. Can you tell which prizes came out of which eggs?

Now let's go to Grandma's House!

We made it to Grandma's House. But we still haven't found the big, yellow egg. Do you see it?

Yeah, there it is!
There's another big egg. But it doesn't look like the others. Who could be inside that egg?

It's Swiper! He'll try to swipe he egg. Say, "Swiper, no swiping!"

Did we find all the eggs? Let's count them in Spanish and see:
uno, dos, tres, cuatro, cinco, seis, siete,
ocho, nueve, diez, once, doce.
Twelve—we did it!

Now we can open the big, yellow egg. It's got the biggest prize of all. Can you guess what's inside?

Hooray! We did it! Look at all the treats that were
inside the big, yellow egg!

We had such an exciting egg hunt today. What was your favorite part? We couldn't have done it without you. Thanks for helping!